This Walker book belongs to:

. . . .

. . . .

. . . .

For Lon and the baby ~ A.H.

For my brother, John ~ H.O.

First published 2013 by Walker Books Ltd
87 Vauxhall Walk, London SE11 5HJ

This edition published 2014

2 4 6 8 10 9 7 5 3 1

Text © 2013 Amy Hest
Illustrations © 2013 Helen Oxenbury

The right of Amy Hest and Helen Oxenbury to be identified as
author and illustrator respectively of this work has been asserted by them
in accordance with the Copyright, Designs and Patents Act 1988

This book has been typeset in Aged

Printed in China

British Library Cataloguing in Publication Data:
a catalogue record for this book is available from the British Library

ISBN 978-1-4063-5566-6

www.walker.co.uk

When Charley Met Granpa

illustrated by

Amy Hest   Helen Oxenbury

WALKER BOOKS
AND SUBSIDIARIES
LONDON • BOSTON • SYDNEY • AUCKLAND

Dear Granpa,

We got a dog. His name is Charley.
He sleeps in my room. He's a fast runner
like me and he's got the same last name
as me, Korn.

When are you coming to see Charley?
Bring a big suitcase and stay a long time
and I'll meet you at the station. My coat has
a hood. Look for a boy waving, that's me.

Love, Henry

Dear Henry,

I'll be there, Sunday, and my train arrives at noon. My suitcase is big. Look for a granpa waving, that's me.

Now, about that dog. Is he friendly or fierce? I've never been friends with a dog before. I'll do my best, but no promises.

Love, Granpa

Sunday was snowy and Charley loves
a snowy day and he loves to go where
I go, so I called through the house,
"Come on, Charley boy!
Come on with me to the station!"

It's two long roads and two short roads from my house to the station. "Wait till you meet Granpa," I told Charley, and he danced in the wind and his ears blew back and I pulled my sled for Granpa's suitcase. New snow was falling over old snow, and Charley's tail was up in the air, which is code for, *I know the way to the station.*

The station looks like a tiny red house,
and there's a bench outside for waiting.
Charley is crazy for trains, just like me,
and waiting for trains, just like me,
and I put my arm around Charley
and we started to wait.

We waited a long time. No whistle. No train.
No Granpa. Snow blew across the tracks, and
we waited some more . . . and some more . . .
and some more. Charley sighed. A lot. He
slid into a sad little slouch. So I talked about
Granpa to make him less sad while we waited.
Charley smiled when I said Granpa's the tallest
Korn with the longest feet and he snores wild.
He did not smile when I said
Granpa doesn't know how
to be friends with a dog.

WHOOOOO WHOOOOOOOO...
Far, far away the train whistle blew.
WHOOO WHOOOOO! Charley's ears
perked up and he sat straight up and I held
on tight – really, really tight – and all of me
shivered and Charley shivered, too.
WHOOOOOOO
WHOOOOOOOOO...
WHOOOOO
WHOOOOOOOO...

Granpa stepped onto the platform.

He waved and waved.

His cap was green.

"Here's Charley," I said. Granpa looked
at Charley, and Charley looked back.
A long time passed.

"Well," said Granpa,
"are you friendly or fierce?"
Charley barked once and smiled.
Granpa did not smile back.

Charley barked at the train for a while,
and when it was gone, he held his
head tall, which is code for, *Follow me,
gentlemen! I know the way home!*

The snow was deep to Charley's knees, and more snow came down. Faster! Whiter! Faster! Then Granpa's cap blew off! Spinning higher! Smaller! Higher! Smaller . . . smaller. . .

Charley chased the cap in the white
whirling snow. Chasing! Chasing!
And then he was gone.
CHARLEY WAS GONE!
"CHARLEY! CHARLEY!
CHARLEYYYYY!"
I was spinning in the wind,
and Granpa was, too, calling,
"CHARLEY! CHARLEY BOY,
COME BACK!"

And then he was there.

With Granpa's

green cap.

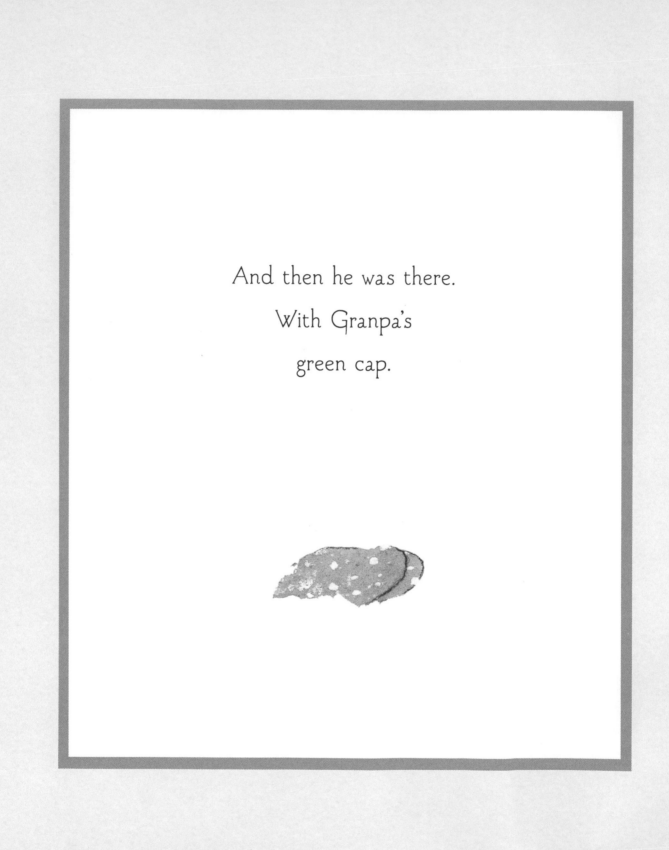

Granpa looked at Charley and Charley
looked back. A long time passed.
Granpa spoke first. "Here you are,"
he said, and then he said, "Nice to meet
you, my friend." The wind blew the snow
and Charley kept the cap.

That night Charley jumped on the bed
with Granpa. He looked in Granpa's
eyes and Granpa looked back,
which is code for,

I love you,

I love you,

I love you.

They both fell asleep.
And Granpa snored wild.

AMY HEST is the author of more than forty books for young readers, for which she has won many awards, from the prestigious Christopher Medal to the Boston Globe Book Award. "I simply write the stories I would have wanted to read when I was a child," she says. Amy lives in New York.

HELEN OXENBURY is among the most popular and critically acclaimed illustrators of her time, winner of the Smarties Book Prize, the Kate Greenaway Medal and the prestigious Kurt Maschler Award. Of the process of illustration, she says, "It's like reading a good book – you don't want it to end." Helen lives in London.

By the same author and illustrator:

Available from all good booksellers

www.walker.co.uk